Cameron loves to get lost in a book or in writing one of his own. Inspiration for his work can come from the smallest of things but with his vivid imagination it often leads to an extraordinary story.

He enjoys working on fictional and fantasy work as this gives him the most freedom and lets him create a world and characters that no one has heard of or seen before.

That's the joy that Cameron finds in books: you can lose yourself in the pages.

MY LITTLE
DRAGON

CAMERON
RHYS JONES

AUSTIN MACAULEY PUBLISHERS™

LONDON • CAMBRIDGE • NEW YORK • SHARJAH

A CIP catalogue record for this title is available from the British Library.

ISBN 9781398411692 (Paperback)
ISBN 9781398411708 (ePub e-book)

www.austinmacauley.com

First Published 2022
Austin Macauley Publishers Ltd®
1 Canada Square
Canary Wharf
London
E14 5AA

I would like to thank Sarah Gabriel, Tom Roberts and Georgia Thomas for helping me fine-tune my work and being ever-supportive of my efforts.

Introduction

Everyone at some time or another has been afraid, be it of spiders, flies, or circus clowns. For young Joseph Smith, it was the sounds he'd hear in the dead of night.
So let me tell you his story, a story of danger, fear, friendship, and just a little bit of magic.

Oh! And, of course, there is the small matter of a dragon.

Chapter 1

I've just told you about the who, what and when; now I suppose I'd better tell you the rest of our story starting with the where. Joseph Smith lived in a little farmhouse in the countryside with his grandfather. The house and farm were one of many dotted about the hillside around them.

Their farmhouse however stood out from the others. Theirs was very different to the plain stonewalls and blandly painted windowsills of the other farmhouses. It had painted white walls and under each windowsill was a box overflowing with colourful flowers.

All in all, it was a rather beautiful little farmhouse.

Joseph was making his way along the winding path to his home. As he got to the side door, he could hear his grandfather calling.

Joseph's grandfather was old. His hair had turned grey and his face had wrinkled but all the years of working on the farm had kept him strong.

Old age however does take its toll, his grandfather was deaf in one ear and his hearing was poor in the other, which meant Joseph had to speak rather loudly all the time for his grandfather to hear him. That didn't matter a bit to Joseph, he loved his grandfather and he knew that his grandfather loved him.

"What took you so long, boy, I thought you'd gotten lost," joked his grandfather. Joseph stepped through the open door into the kitchen and placed the eggs he'd collected on the kitchen table.

"I didn't want to drop the eggs, so I took my time," replied Joseph, taking his seat at the table as his grandfather got everything ready for breakfast.

"Hmmm," mumbled his grandfather, having a sip of his coffee with one hand, as he scrambled the eggs with the other.

"One of the sheep got out last night, and not only that, it broke a section of the fence on its way out," said Joseph's grandfather as he took a seat by the table.
"What part of the fence?" asked Joseph before taking a bite of toast.

"It was one of the sections near the forest. I couldn't see the sheep on the path this morning, so I can only assume that it wandered into the forest for some reason," said his grandfather before having another sip of coffee and taking a bite of toast himself.

"Will we go looking for it in the forest?" As Joseph asked the question his heart raced a little, afraid of what the answer would be.
"No, no, we have no idea what time the sheep got out; it could be miles away by now. With a bit of luck, it might wander onto one of the other farms nearby and the farmer will bring her back to us," replied his grandfather.

"Okay, Granddad," said Joseph, thankful his grandfather hadn't said yes, the forest had always made Joseph feel uneasy. He always felt as though something was watching him from behind the trees, just waiting for him to wonder a little closer before grabbing him.

Joseph tried to push the forest to the back of his mind and after finishing breakfast, Joseph set about clearing the table as he always did. He wasn't really paying attention to what he was doing, however, he had other things on his mind.
"Watch out for the plate!" But it was too late, the plate went crashing to the floor.
"I'm sorry, Granddad, I'll clear it up," said Joseph in a solemn tone.
"It's only a plate, Joseph," said his grandfather, as he placed a caring hand on Joseph's shoulder.
"Are you sure you're okay, Joseph, your mind seems to be elsewhere lately, is something the matter?"
asked his grandfather.

Joseph wanted to tell his grandfather what was bothering him. He wanted to tell him about the awful sounds he'd been hearing in the night, but he didn't want to worry his grandfather. Also, he knew that his grandfather wouldn't have heard the sounds because of his hearing. So, Joseph kept what had been happening to himself.

"I'm fine, Granddad; I just wasn't paying attention to what I was doing. I was, ugh... thinking about how to fix the fence," said Joseph, trying his best to mask his fear. "Okay, Joseph, it's nice to see you're so eager to help. Let's get to fixing that fence then," said his grandfather with a grin. Joseph could see however that his grandfather didn't quite believe him, but he also knew his grandfather wouldn't push him to speak if he didn't want to.

They made their way to the front door where Joseph helped his grandfather put on his old leather boots, before putting on his own much newer pair of boots.

 14

Joseph and his grandfather then set off towards the broken section of the fence.

Tool Box

The whole time they were fixing the fence, Joseph still felt like he was being watched.

Joseph tried his best to ignore this feeling, but he was still relieved when they'd finished so that they could move away from the forest and away from those hidden eyes. The rest of Joseph's day was spent cleaning up after the animals and making sure their pens were ready for the night.

"I think you've done enough for today, Joseph, why don't you head back to the house and get yourself ready for bed, I'll be along once I've finished here," said Joseph's grandfather after stretching out his back.

Joseph did as his grandfather asked and made his way back to the house, glancing back every so often to check on his grandfather to make sure he was ok.

Joseph opened the wooden doors to the house; stepping inside, he kicked off his muddy boots and put them neatly on the shoe rack. He went upstairs to have a

wash, brush his teeth and change into his pyjamas. As he was laying out his clothes for tomorrow, he heard his grandfather come in through the front door. Joseph went downstairs to help his grandfather take off his boots. Joseph always laughed at the noises his grandfather would make as he pulled at the boots.

After his grandfather had washed and changed, the pair then sat by the open log fire: his grandfather in the old leather armchair and Joseph on his pile of mismatched pillows on the floor. Joseph's grandfather took a book off the shelf and started reading to Joseph as he often did. His grandfather told the best stories. He didn't always read his stories from a book either. Sometimes he'd just start telling a story that he was once told as a boy, those were the stories that Joseph loved the most.

Some days it would be about wild beasts and wilder men, others it would be knights in armour fighting for their kingdom.
It didn't really matter what it was about, his grandfather made them all
come alive.

The time seemed to fly by and before Joseph knew it, the clock chimed for 9:00 pm and he knew that the story

however great, would have to wait
for tomorrow.
"Well then, Joseph, it's time for us to turn in
for the night. We've got a long day's work
ahead of us tomorrow; come on, I'll race you
to the top of the stairs,"
said his grandfather.

Joseph scurried to his feet and bounded for
the stairs; he raced up but stopped near the
top to let his grandfather catch up before
reaching the landing.

"I'll beat you one day," said his grandfather
as he rustled Joseph's hair with his hand.
Joseph and his grandfather made their way
down the hall to Joseph's bedroom.

His room was like any other, a single bed
covered in thick warm duvets. At either side
of his bed, a nightstand made of oak and
at the bottom of his bed was a rather large
toy chest, again made of oak but with a
colourful fabric top. Much like the rest of the

house, his room was warm and cosy. They walked together to his bed, Joseph climbed in and his grandfather tucked him under the duvets.

"Goodnight, sleep tight and I'll see you in the morning," said his grandfather as he made his way out of the room. He stopped at the door, turned off the light, and with one last smile, he closed the door behind him.

As soon as the door had closed, Joseph threw off his duvets and rushed to lock the bedroom door. Once the door was locked, Joseph returned to his bed where he lay motionless, waiting for darkness to come. The orange light from the sun outside his window faded moment by moment until it was replaced with the black of night.

As he lay there waiting, he grew tenser and tenser. He was afraid that the sounds he'd been hearing in the night would return again tonight, and there was nothing he could do besides wait and hope they wouldn't come.

20

Every night, since the sounds had started, they seemed to be drawing closer to him. Tonight was no different. The sounds started echoing around his room, sounding closer to the farm than they had yesterday.
Closer to him.
He hid under the covers hoping the sounds wouldn't find him. He heard the crack of wood splintering; the sounds were so very loud now. Frozen with fear, he held his breath; he didn't dare get up to look out his window because he was afraid of what he would see out there in the dark.

Then, almost as quickly as they had started, the sounds began to fade away. Joseph couldn't rest however, what if the sounds came back for him while he slept? He was on edge until the orange light of dawn started gently seeping through his window. Joseph didn't know why but whatever the sounds were, they didn't like the daytime, and they always fell silent as the sun rose. Now that he felt safer, Joseph fell into an exhausted sleep.

Chapter 2

Just a few hours later, Joseph's grandfather was knocking at his bedroom door.

"Are you going to sleep all day, Joseph?" he called out jokingly from behind the door. "We really do have another busy day ahead of us. Another one of the sheep managed to get out of the pen last night, but this time it completely shattered a section of the fence, top and bottom rail, I don't know what's got into those sheep," his grandfather sighed. "Come on, your breakfast is getting cold."

Joseph, exhausted from his poor night's sleep got dressed, unlocked his bedroom door and then thudded down the stairs towards the kitchen.
"Are you feeling well, Joseph?" asked his grandfather. "You look very tired." His grandfather's eyes were full of worry.

22

It was at this point that Joseph's emotions got the better of him and he broke down in floods of tears. With his head in his hands and in-between the snobs and the sniffles, Joseph explained to his grandfather what he'd been hearing during the nights. His grandfather sat by the table listening intently to what Joseph had to say.

"Hmmm, I see, well, we can't have that now, can we?" His grandfather got up from the table and walked over to Joseph.
"Stay here a moment, I'm just going to pop upstairs and get something for you." His grandfather sounded as though he had the very thing that would solve the problem, just lying around upstairs.

After a minute or so, Joseph heard his grandfather making his way back down the stairs. He appeared at the door with something in his hands—a small wooden box. It was made of deep red wood and around its edges were intertwined silver threads that seemed to almost shimmer in the light; it was oh so beautiful. As Joseph's grandfather sat next to him, Joseph noticed that on the lid of the box was a carving, a carving of a dragon. Joseph sat there in awe of the box; his imagination was running wild as to what could be inside.

"Well, go on then, it's not going to open by itself, is it?" his grandfather teased as he handed Joseph the box.

Slowly, Joseph opened the lid of the box. As he did a wave seemed to wash over him. All his worry and fear simply melted away as if by magic. Peeking inside, Joseph saw what appeared to be a small toy dragon, but it wasn't like anything else he'd seen before. The dragon had rose gold scales that seemed to flicker in the light, and its eyes were a deep ruby red.

Carefully, Joseph took the dragon from the box and held it in his hand. To his surprise, the dragon gave off a gentle warmth and the feeling that had washed over him as he opened the box, grew stronger and stronger. Only one thing worried Joseph as he held the dragon in his hand, he was sure that he could feel it moving. It couldn't be, he thought to himself, I'm just tired and imagining things.

Joseph's grandfather took him by the shoulder and said, "My grandfather gave him to me when I was about your age. Not that you'd believe it but even I've been afraid from time to time. So I'll tell you the same thing my grandfather told me when he gave me that dragon. He said to me, 'This dragon is very special; during the day, he'll sleep and you have to look after him but during the night the dragon will look after you. He will keep you safe and protect you, but there are some rules you have to follow mind you.'"

Bubbling with excitement, Joseph asked his grandfather, "What are they? I'll make sure that I follow them all." He didn't quite understand what his grandfather meant by 'the dragon will look after you' but Joseph liked the idea of having his own dragon, even if it was only a toy.

"Rule number one, during the day you have to look after the dragon. You'll have to make sure he's kept clean and put back near his box at the end of the day," said his grandfather, holding up a finger.

"Rule number two, you have to leave your door unlocked in the nights, so the dragon can come back in easily," said his grandfather, raising another finger.

"And the third and final rule, you can't follow the dragon during the night no matter what. If you can stick to those three rules the dragon will always look after you," said his grandfather as he wiggled all three of his fingers.

"Granddad, I don't understand the last two rules. Surely the dragon can't move, it's just a toy, isn't it?" asked Joseph.

"You'll just have to wait and see, won't you?" his grandfather chuckled. "Now, take him up to your room for safekeeping. As I said, we have a busy day today and we can't waste it chatting away."

Joseph did as his grandfather said and took the box that held the little dragon to his room and put it on his bedside table. He took one last look inside at the dragon, closed the lid and set off to meet his grandfather who was already making his way over to the broken fence.

"I just can't make sense of it, Joseph," said his grandfather as he laid down his tools and the new beam for the fence.

"What's that, Granddad?"

"Those beams are quite thick. A sheep shouldn't be able to break through them easily. That's the whole point of the fence after all." His grandfather stared at the

28

missing section of the fence for a moment or so, trying to figure out what could have happened during the night.

"Ah, I'm probably overthinking things in my old age. The beam was likely rotten which is why it broke so easily. Enough of my rambling, could you pass me the measuring tape, please, Joseph?"

The pair's day was filled with fixing the broken section of the fence and tending to the day-to-day chores around the farm. As they finished their final chore, the sun was beginning to slowly set; the sky was still blue but now a dark blue.

They were so tired that they were dragging their feet along the path back to the house. Luckily enough Joseph's grandfather had prepared their dinner that morning, just in case they were too tired after a hard day's work. And that they were.

After their evening meal, Joseph and his grandfather spent some time reading in the living room. His grandfather could see how tired he was, Joseph's grandfather laid down his book, "Thank you for all your help today, I don't think I could have gotten everything done without you. Now why don't you go and get ready for bed, I'll tidy up down here."

Although Joseph loved spending time reading with his grandfather, he could feel his eyes getting heavy. Joseph stood up and yawned, the hard day's work had really caught up to him. He could only manage to mumble, "Okay, Granddad, goodnight," as he trudged his way to the stairs.

Joseph set about his nightly routine, washing his face, brushing his teeth and setting his clothes out ready for tomorrow.
Tonight, however, there was an added step in his routine. He sat on the edge of his bed and opened the box that his grandfather had given him, and there inside
was his little dragon. That special wave washed over Joseph again and he didn't feel as tired anymore.

He picked up the dragon and started cleaning it with the polishing cloth that was at the bottom of the box.

He must have been there for over half an hour cleaning the dragon until it shone all over from head to tail.

31

"Are you still up, Joseph?" asked his grandfather, poking his head around the door. "I thought you'd be fast asleep by now ahhh, I see, I thought you might have forgotten about the first rule. I think that's the cleanest I've ever seen that Joseph," he chuckled. "It's about time for bed, go on jump in, I'll get the light for you. Goodnight, Joseph."

"Goodnight, Granddad," replied Joseph, as he put the dragon back on the side table. Joseph snuggled into bed while his grandfather turned the light off and closed the door. Joseph could hear him walking away and then heard the unmistakable thud of his grandfather's bedroom door as it closed. With that, the house fell silent and his room turned dark.

However, not as dark as it normally did, there was a faint glow in the room and that glow was coming from his dragon! Joseph slowly reached from his bed and picked up his dragon as he did the glow got brighter. He'd never seen anything so mesmerising; his little dragon was beautiful.

Joseph was overflowing with excitement, he wanted to run and show his grandfather, but just as he was getting up from his bed...the sounds started their awful chorus once again! Pulling the duvet back over himself Joseph hid under the covers, his dragon in hand.

Joseph had forgotten about the sounds because of his dragon but the sounds hadn't forgotten about him. They always started when it was dark outside. It was like some great beast would rise as the sun set and when it did, it was hungry and looking for fresh meat.

Joseph's heart was racing; he closed his eyes and tried not to listen to the sounds that were getting ever louder.

"Why won't they leave me alone?" he whispered holding the duvet with one hand and his dragon in the other.

Joseph lay there under the duvet, his eyes shut tightly, trembling with fear, but something made him open his eyes and that something almost made him leap from the bed.

The dragon in his hand was moving!

Chapter 3

The dragon was actually moving and wriggling around in his hand!

Joseph opened his hand and the dragon rolled onto the bed, it stretched its body, shook its head and began to sniff at Joseph. The world outside of Joseph's bedroom seemed to fall away. It was just Joseph and his dragon.

"Hello, m-my name's Joseph," he whispered to the dragon, holding out his hand. The dragon took another sniff of Joseph and then started to nudge his hand affectionately, so Joseph started to pet his dragon. Joseph hadn't felt this safe in a long time, he felt warm right down to his bones and felt like he didn't have a care in the world. That was until there was a loud crack of wood splintering which almost made Joseph jump

out of his skin. The sounds had
drawn nearer.

This sent his dragon into a frenzy. It
wriggled its way out from under the duvet
and leapt off the bed towards the window,
landing gently on the windowsill. It nudged
open the window and sniffed at the
night air.

Joseph leapt out of bed after his dragon.
"Wait, you can't go out there, the sounds
are out there," said Joseph, his voice
full of fear.

The dragon turned to Joseph and gave
him a smile, well, at least Joseph thought it
was a smile, and then it jumped out of the
window. Joseph rushed to the window and
saw his dragon flying through the air, its
wings glinting in the starlight. It landed on
the fence outside his home. Then just like a
flash of lightning, the dragon bolted towards
the forest.

Joseph rushed to the other side of the room and started putting his clothes on, he was going to go after the dragon but he stopped just as he got his left sock on, one of the rules his grandfather had told him stopped him in his tracks.

'You can't follow the dragon during the night no matter what.'
Joseph paused for a moment then heard a loud roar, louder than anything he'd heard so far. It sounded like the cry of some wounded beast echoing through the
night air.

He went back to the window to see if he could see the dragon. He could see something in the distance, a faint glow moving through the forest. That must be my dragon, he thought, breathing a sigh of relief. Whatever is making the sounds hadn't gotten him yet. It was then that Joseph noticed something, the sounds had become quieter as if they were further away. Whatever the dragon was doing, it was working.

Within the hour, the sounds had completely vanished. His dragon had done it. Joseph could see that the glow was getting brighter and sure enough, his dragon came into view. Joseph was so happy he could barely contain himself, the sounds were finally gone and it was all thanks to his dragon.

Joseph left the window open for the dragon to get back in. He also made sure that his bedroom door was unlocked just in case, Rule 2, he thought. Joseph strolled back to his bed with a joyful swagger and collapsed face-first into it. This was going to be the best night's sleep he'd had in a long time and he wasn't going to waste a second of it, and as his head hit the pillow, he fell into a blissfully deep sleep.

Joseph woke to streams of light flooding through his window. He'd almost forgotten what it was like to wake up well-rested and ready for the day. He took possibly the biggest stretch he'd ever taken and then looked around the room, and there atop its box was his dragon. Joseph went to speak to the dragon but then he remembered what his grandfather had said, 'He sleeps during the day,' so he just smiled at it and then rolled himself out of bed. He was so excited to tell his grandfather what had happened during the night. He was bounding around his room getting ready. He was just about to leave his room when he stopped and turned to look at his dragon.

"You looked after me in the night, so I'll look after you in the day," declared Joseph. "I'll show you around the farm so that you know what everything looks like."
Joseph put the dragon in his jacket pocket and went downstairs. His grandfather was in the kitchen making breakfast, scrambled eggs on toast.

"Granddad, Granddad," yelled Joseph. "It came to life, the dragon actually came to life and it stopped those awful sounds. It ran off into the forest in the night and the sounds, they just stopped," said Joseph, bubbling with excitement.

"Well, I did tell you that it was special after all, didn't I?" said his grandfather. "Don't forget about the rules though, Joseph, they are very important if you want to keep that dragon. I know you said that you wouldn't forget but I thought I'd just remind you from time to time."

"I won't forget, Granddad, I'll look after him and keep him clean, I won't follow him and I'll leave my door unlocked," said Joseph, reciting the rules back to his grandfather to show he hadn't forgotten.

"That's good to know," his grandfather smiled. "It's just our normal chores around the farm that need doing today. But before all of that, first things first, breakfast," said his grandfather as he put Joseph's plate on the table.

They finished their breakfast and went out to tend to the farm. They may have gotten their chores done a little faster but throughout the day, Joseph took his dragon from his pocket and showed it what he was doing, and how to get back to the house from where they were. Joseph wasn't sure if the dragon would remember, but he couldn't see the harm in showing him and his grandfather didn't seem to mind at all.

As the day drew to a close, Joseph was looking forward to laying down for a long night's sleep. He knew that now he had his dragon, he'd sleep soundly. He was almost skipping and jumping back to the house when they'd finished their work for the day. Joseph helped his grandfather take off his boots and then went to get washed and changed.

The pair spent some time in the living room doing a little reading before bed, as they always did.

41

After cleaning his dragon by the fire, Joseph could feel his eyes getting heavy, so he said goodnight to his grandfather and made his way to his room.

"I'll be up soon, Joseph, I just want to finish this chapter," said his grandfather, raising his book into the air.
Joseph had just curled up under his duvet, as he did his grandfather popped his head around the door.

"Goodnight, Joseph, see you in the morning."

"Goodnight, Granddad," replied Joseph. His grandfather turned off his bedroom light and then closed the bedroom door behind him. Joseph turned to his dragon, "Goodnight, Dragon," he said with a smile before settling down for the night.

It wasn't long before Joseph fell into what he thought would be an uneventful night's sleep.
Oh, how wrong he was.
Startled, Joseph woke from his sleep. The awful sounds were back.

He didn't know what to do, he was beginning to panic, he could feel himself shaking, but then a familiar warmth washed over him. His dragon was glowing as it had before; leaping into action once again, it bounded towards the window, towards those awful sounds.

The dragon dashed towards the forest glowing like hot coals. It was heading towards the sounds as it had before but this time, the sounds didn't get quieter, this time they got louder, they seemed to be almost taunting the dragon to come and find them.
It was a minute or so after his dragon had entered the forest that Joseph heard a crack like thunder and his dragon's light went out.

Chapter 4

Joseph blinked wildly and then scanned every inch of the dark outside his window. He couldn't see the light from his dragon. He stared into the darkness hoping to catch a glimpse of the light from his dragon, but he saw nothing. Panic took hold of Joseph; he could do nothing but stand there and think about what had happened to his dragon out in the dark.

It seemed as though hours had passed since the light from his dragon went out, but then a faint glow appeared in the forest.
"My dragon," said Joseph, leaping into the air. He was so happy to see that glow; his dragon was okay.

After a few seconds, however, he realised that the glow wasn't moving, it was staying in the forest. He knew then that something was wrong.

Maybe he's hurt or maybe, something's stopping him from coming home, thought Joseph. His fear started to bubble at the back of his mind again.

Turning from the window, Joseph started putting his clothes on. Even though he was afraid, he wasn't going to leave his friend alone out there in the dark. He didn't know how he was going to help his dragon but he had to try to help his friend. Joseph crept down the stairs and made his way to the front door. He knew his grandfather wouldn't hear him, but he crept all the same.

He stood in the doorway of the house looking out at the forest to where the glow was flickering between the trees. Joseph hesitated to step out into the night. He knew he'd be breaking one of the rules he told his grandfather he would stick to if he did.

An awful feeling came over Joseph. He was almost afraid to move, but Joseph straightened his back and said aloud, "I have to do something. I can't leave him out there alone in the dark," he grabbed the torch that was by the front door and set off into the night towards the forest, and towards his dragon.

As Joseph moved through the farmyard toward the forest, he could hear the crows squawking and screaming at each other.

They seemed to be almost laughing at him as he moved deeper into the night. As he got closer to the forest, he could hear the trees creaking as they bent in the wind. Joseph tightened his grip around his torch and pushed on trying his best to ignore the crows and the trees, but there was one

thing he couldn't ignore, the awful sounds coming from the direction of the glow, the direction of his dragon.

He'd spent so many nights now being terrified of those sounds, afraid they'd find him and now he was walking straight towards them. Of course, he was afraid but he had to keep going, he had to find his dragon.

Before long, Joseph found himself at the edge of the forest. He knew he was getting closer to the sounds but he was also getting closer to his dragon. So he took a deep breath and headed into the forest. He walked carefully to avoid the twisted tree roots that were just waiting to grab him as he made his way forward.

Scanning the forest before him with his torch, Joseph saw a kind of mist rising from behind a small mound in front of him.

He couldn't see what was causing it, but the glow was much brighter there, it had to be his dragon.

Joseph rushed forward but as he got to the top of the mound, he stumbled over a root and fell into the dirt with a thud.

He was about to pick himself up when he looked forward and saw a fire. He lay there motionless in the dirt. The glow he'd been following wasn't his dragon; it was the glow from a fire!

Hanging over the fire was a large black cauldron and rising from the cauldron was a thick haze of smoke that seemed to hang in the air. Bubbling over the edge of the cauldron was a foul-looking black slurry that seemed to be churning all on its own. Crawling slowly through the dirt, Joseph moved forward to get a better look. As he did, he could smell whatever it was that was cooking in the cauldron, and it was the foulest thing Joseph had ever smelt, and living on a farm he'd smelt a lot. Joseph could still hear the awful sounds but now they were much clearer, he could have sworn that they sounded like someone mumbling, just like his granddad would do from time to time, only far more twisted and frightening.

He still couldn't see what was making the sounds and he was thankful for that in a way. He didn't really want to know.

Just off to the side of the cauldron next to an uprooted tree that had been partially chopped to pieces, was a large wooden chest. The chest was covered with thick iron chains and a large lock was holding all the chains together, keeping the chest shut. As he watched the chest, he could see it shuddering every so often.

As Joseph lay there in the dirt, he began to hear a banging sound coming from inside, as if something was trying to get out, trying to escape.

It then dawned on Joseph that it could be his dragon trapped in the chest.

"My dragon," said Joseph, leaping to his feet. "Don't worry, Dragon, I'm coming. I'll get you out of there," he shouted. Covering his mouth and nose with his sleeve to avoid breathing in the foul stench that was coming from the cauldron, Joseph rushed towards the chest. Pulling, twisting and bashing at the chains, Joseph tried to open the chest, but nothing worked. The chains were too thick, and Joseph was too small.

Looking around for something to help, he grabbed a branch from the fallen tree and wedged it into the lock and put all of his weight against it, the branch simply splintered.

He was sure now that his dragon was inside the chest. He could feel warmth coming from inside that could only be his dragon. As Joseph stood next to the chest, he realised that whilst he'd been trying to open the chest the awful sounds had disappeared,

only the sound of the forest kept him
company now. Joseph stopped and listened,
maybe they had just decided to go away,
he thought, hoping that was the truth. It
was then he heard it, the sound of heavy
breathing coming from behind him.
Slowly, Joseph turned to face the sound,
fearing what would be behind him. As he
stared into the forest, Joseph saw two
yellow eyes staring back at him.

The creature stepped into the light of the
clearing and Joseph realised with horror that
he recognised what it was. This monstrous
creature was a troll, just like from the
stories that his grandfather had
read to him.

The troll must have been 10 feet away but
even from that distance, Joseph knew two
things for sure.

One, it was huge, it must have been as big as a barn door and two, it smelt worse than the slurry pouring out of the cauldron.
The troll took two long strides on its giant legs and stood towering in front of Joseph, its feet stopping just inches from his own. "Well, what do we 'ave 'ere?" snarled the troll as he bent down to inspect Joseph. As it did, Joseph saw the troll's teeth, rotten and riddled with mould.

The troll had greenish-grey skin and a tattered cloth covering its waist. Its arms and legs bulged with muscle while its belly was large and round.

Not something you'd like to find in your back garden that's for sure, and certainly not something you'd want to be as close to as Joseph found himself now.

Chapter 5

Joseph could feel himself shaking as he stood face to face with this giant, hideous creature.

"I'm I'm looking for my dragon, I think he's in your chest, Sir," squeaked Joseph, trying to be as brave as he could.

The troll boomed with laughter. "That little pest is yours! That thing ran me ragged last night. It chased me to the edge of the forest, only when I was some miles away from here did it stop. It almost made me want to move on from this place and find somewhere else to feed, but the food you have here is mmmmm so juicy," the troll was slobbering as it spoke. Joseph hadn't moved a muscle since the troll had lunged up to him. He'd thought about trying to run and get help, but he knew that he wouldn't be able to outrun the troll; he'd just seen how fast it could move.

"I couldn't believe my luck when I stumbled upon these hills," said the troll, gesturing to the world around him. "There are so many different farms with so many different animals, I mean who was going to notice a chicken here and a sheep there," grinned the troll, "And the last thing I'm going to let me stop from enjoying such a feast is that little pest." The troll kicked the chest, tipping it on its side, the chains still held fast.

"Please let him go," cried Joseph. "He won't bother you anymore, I'll keep him away from the forest, please, just let him go!"
The troll boomed with laughter yet again, but this time he stooped to laugh in Joseph's face; its breath was so pungent it made Joseph's eyes burn.

"You want me to let that thing go, and have it go chasing me around the forest again? You have no chance of that, little boy. I'll not have that thing trying to burn me out of this forest again," said the troll, crossing its arms.
"What do you mean, burn you?" Joseph

cried out. "It's not a real dragon, it doesn't breathe fire, it's just a toy." Joseph was trying his best to keep the troll talking. He didn't know what good it would do, but he couldn't think of anything else to do. Lucky for Joseph, the troll seemed all too happy to talk and tell Joseph about its troubles.

"No, it doesn't breathe fire, but its scales are hotter than anything I can bear. I could feel the heat it was giving off as it was coming closer and closer to me, us trolls don't do well with heat that's why we stay out of the sunlight," the troll stooped down and rolled up a bandage that it had on its left arm. Joseph could see that the skin was cracked and burnt.

"That's what the little pest did to me last night when I tried to swat it away. So tonight, I set a trap for it and here we are, it's trapped in a chest, and its owner's come to join it," the troll smiled a toothy grin. "I was going to dump that dragon of yours

into the cauldron, chest and all but I better check that it's hot enough first," mused the troll as it held its chin with its hand. "Hmm, I think I'll test it with you."

Joseph tried to run but the troll was too fast, it took him in its hand and hoisted him into the air as if he was as light as a feather.

"Maybe I'll just cook you up and eat you instead, it's been quite some time since I've had people for tea," laughed the troll. Joseph wriggled and squirmed, trying his best to break free from the troll's grip. "Let me go," he cried, "you can't do this to people, HELP!"

"Quit your moaning. No one or nothing's going to come and help you now," the troll turned and dangled Joseph over the cauldron, Joseph could see the slurry churning and bubbling beneath him. He could do nothing but cry out for help.
It was then Joseph heard it, a roar so loud

it sounded like thunder ringing in his ears. The troll turned on its heels to face the sound, with Joseph dangling at his side still some feet off the ground. The sound came again, only this time much, much louder. It was coming from the chest, coming from his dragon. The troll leant into the chest to make sure the chains were steady, as he did, a third roar boomed. This time Joseph's dragon burst from the chest glowing so brightly the air around it seemed to shimmer.

The troll recoiled from the light as though he'd been woken from a deep slumber by the searchlight of a ship. Shielding its eyes from the light, it dropped Joseph who fell to the ground with a thud. Luckily for Joseph, he'd landed in a moss patch, and not on the roots of a tree. Joseph's dragon then leapt at the troll knocking it into the cauldron, spilling the black slurry everywhere. The troll wreathed in pain as it staggered

back to its feet. "It burns, it burns!" it cried. "I'll make you pay for this!" yelled the troll as it fixed its eyes on Joseph. The troll then charged at him.

Joseph's dragon moved faster than anything he'd ever seen. Before the troll had taken its second stride, his dragon stood between them and the troll stopped in its tracks. Joseph was stood some way from his dragon, but he could still feel the waves of heat washing over him as he had done before, but it was much stronger now.

"I BEAT YOU ONCE, I'LL BEAT YOU AGAIN," yelled the troll, raising its fist in the air.

Joseph's dragon turned to face him, its mouth didn't move but Joseph could hear its voice, "Thank you for coming to save me, Joseph now run home. I'll take care of this brute." The dragon turned to face the troll once more.

"You can talk?" muttered Joseph in complete amazement

"Yes, Joseph. Now please, RUN!" with that final word, the dragon leapt at the troll, sending it tumbling deeper into the forest, his dragon roared and gave chase, its glow illuminating the darkness around it.

Joseph was about to chase after his dragon but he stopped himself. He knew if he followed his dragon he'd just be putting them both in more danger, so he did as his dragon had asked and ran home as fast as his feet would carry him. He could hear his dragon and the troll fighting behind him but he did not look back, he pushed on through the forest towards home.

The forest grew darker away from the light of the fire. Joseph had dropped his torch in panic, but his eyes had got used to the dark, so he managed to get out of the forest without falling on the roots that had snagged him before. As he broke through the tree line, the farm opened up before him. It was bathed in a pale moonlight, which made it a bit easier for Joseph to see.

From behind him, he heard a roar so loud it made the very ground shake, the troll wasn't going to give up so easily. Joseph heard the crashing of rocks and the splintering of trees. The troll was throwing everything it could at the dragon.

What if he does beat my dragon? The thought made Joseph's fear start to well up in him once more.

Joseph ran back to the house along the dirt path. He was shaking at the thought of that beast beating his dragon and then finding its way back to the farm. He fumbled at the latch to the front door; he could feel the panic rising inside him. He spun his head around expecting to find the troll standing behind him, but the only thing behind him was the farm. The latch finally gave way and Joseph burst inside and rushed upstairs. Even through the walls of his house, he heard another roar, even louder than before, then an eerie silence filled the air.

He darted into his room and closed the bedroom door, locking it behind him for what good it would do (a mistake that he wouldn't notice until the morning). He ran to the chair by the window and stared into the night for any sign of his dragon. He waited and waited as the minutes turned into hours with no sign of his dragon or the troll. Exhausted, unable to stay awake, Joseph fell into a troubled, restless sleep.

Chapter 6

Joseph woke to streams of light dancing through the window and birds singing their merry songs, it would seem that the troll hadn't followed him after all. He examined the farm from his window. All of the fences looked to be fine, there were no broken trees nor large footprints in the ground, his dragon had done it. He turned to his bedside expecting to see his dragon sat on its box, but it wasn't there.

Joseph started to tear his bedroom apart looking for his dragon. For the best part of an hour, he searched but he found no sign. He rushed to his bedroom door and tried to open it but the lock held firm, all at once everything Joseph had done the night before came flooding back to him. In his panic last night, he'd locked the door behind him. He hadn't meant to do it; he was just so scared he must have done it without thinking.

His grandfather's words echoed in his ears, 'You have to leave your door unlocked in the nights, so the dragon can come back in easily.' Joseph unlocked the door and swung it open wildly, hoping that his dragon would be on the floor but to his horror it wasn't. Joseph began to cry, he'd left his friend in the forest alone to fight the beast while he ran to save himself. Not only that, he'd then locked his door so that if the dragon had made it back, it wouldn't be able to get in.

What if the dragon thought that I didn't want him anymore and that's why I locked my door on him? thought Joseph as he rushed downstairs, now in streams of tears. His grandfather was sitting at the dinner table facing away from him.

Joseph in fits of tears, coughs and sniffles explained to his grandfather what had happened the night before. He told his grandfather how he had gone out into the night to try and help his dragon, how the troll had almost turned him into a stew and how his dragon had fought the beast off while Joseph ran. After Joseph had finished telling his grandfather what had happened, he noticed that his grandfather hadn't said a word, he had barely moved as a matter of fact.

Joseph fell to his knees. "I'm so sorry I didn't listen to you, Granddad, but I couldn't leave him out there alone, even if he is a dragon. Please can you help me find him, I can try to explain that I do care about him and I didn't mean to lock him out. Please, Granddad, please," sobbed Joseph as he dropped his gaze to the floor.

Joseph heard his grandfather getting up and he felt his hand touch the top of his head. "I'm very proud of you, Joseph," he said. "I am of course upset that you would ignore me and go wandering off at night on your own, but you were very brave going out into

the dark to help your friend. How could I possibly be anything but proud?" He lifted Joseph's head. "Not only that but you were honest enough to tell me the truth about what had happened, knowing full well that I would be upset."

Joseph looked up at his grandfather and he could see that his grandfather was smiling at him.

With watery eyes, Joseph found a smile. "So, you'll help me find him then?" asked Joseph, getting to his feet.

"I won't have to help you, I'm pretty sure you can find him on your own." His grandfather gestured to the countertop where stood on an old tin box was his dragon. Joseph burst into tears again but this time they were tears of happiness.

He rushed over to the counter and took the dragon in his arms. "Where did you find him?"

"Well, when he couldn't get into your room last night, he came to find me instead. I've always kept a spare box by my bedside just in case the wooden one ever broke and a good job I did too," he laughed. "I knew something had happened during the night when I found him there this morning."

Joseph couldn't remember a time when he'd been so happy. He held up his dragon. "I'm sorry about locking you out of my room, I promise it will never happen again," he said softly. The dragon simply winked at him. "Right, now that everything is back in order, it's time for you to do some chores for not listening and wandering off on your own, wouldn't you say, Joseph?" asked his grandfather, raising his eyebrow.

"Of course, I'll just get changed and I'll be right out, Granddad," he said as he made his

way upstairs with his dragon in hand. Joseph met his grandfather outside and set about doing all of the messy tasks around the farm. Mucking out the stables for one, but he didn't complain once because he knew it was a small price to pay for his dragon. His grandfather was helping too, even though he said he wasn't going to. For the days and nights that followed, Joseph and his dragon were inseparable, never far from each other's side. The troll that had been causing so much trouble was never heard from again.

Not in these parts anyway.

And so, Joseph, his grandfather and his dragon went on with their days as normal. Well, as normal as they could be when you have your own dragon to look after. Joseph was no longer afraid of the dark and what could be there. He felt safe knowing that if something like this ever happened again, his dragon would be there for him and he would be there for his dragon.

CPSIA information can be obtained
at www.ICGtesting.com
Printed in the USA
LVHW070720170622
721470LV00014B/349

9 781398 411692